For my excellent nephews, Isaac and Aaron,
who each have within them equal parts Arthur and Merlin, and who,
in their own unique ways, are destined to achieve great things

—J.K.

To my wife, Helen

—I.O.

✦ A WORD ABOUT ARTHUR ✦

The legend of King Arthur has captivated and inspired readers for generations. Arthur was the son of a king who was raised without that knowledge by Sir Ector. During that time England was in turmoil and needed a new leader to unite the people, so the wizard Merlin called forth a sword stuck inside a stone. On the stone was written "He who draws this sword from the stone shall be king." Teenage Arthur drew it out, proving that he was the true and rightful king of England. He became a great and benevolent king, married Princess Guenevere, and relied on Merlin's wisdom and wizardry.

The mystery of how Merlin "called forth" the sword is never made clear. I'm honored to add my own personal piece to the Arthur puzzle by imagining a childhood adventure between Arthur and Guenevere. Whether he lived in real life or only in our minds and hearts, as long as King Arthur continues to inspire humankind to do that which is honorable, decent, and good, then he truly lives in us all.

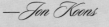

—Jon Koons

DUTTON CHILDREN'S BOOKS • A division of Penguin Young Readers Group
Published by the Penguin Group • Penguin Group (USA) Inc., 375 Hudson Street, New York, New York 10014, U.S.A. • Penguin Group (Canada), 90 Eglinton Avenue East, Suite 700, Toronto, Ontario, Canada M4P 2Y3 (a division of Pearson Penguin Canada Inc.) • Penguin Books Ltd, 80 Strand, London WC2R 0RL, England • Penguin Ireland, 25 St Stephen's Green, Dublin 2, Ireland (a division of Penguin Books Ltd) • Penguin Group (Australia), 250 Camberwell Road, Camberwell, Victoria 3124, Australia (a division of Pearson Australia Group Pty Ltd) • Penguin Books India Pvt Ltd, 11 Community Centre, Panchsheel Park, New Delhi - 110 017, India • Penguin Group (NZ), 67 Apollo Drive, Rosedale, North Shore 0632, New Zealand (a division of Pearson New Zealand Ltd) • Penguin Books (South Africa) (Pty) Ltd, 24 Sturdee Avenue, Rosebank, Johannesburg 2196, South Africa • Penguin Books Ltd, Registered Offices: 80 Strand, London WC2R 0RL, England

Text copyright © 2008 by Jon Koons   Illustrations copyright © 2008 by Igor Oleynikov

Library of Congress Cataloging-in-Publication Data

Koons, Jon.
Arthur and Guen : an original tale of young Camelot / by Jon Koons ; illustrated by Igor Oleynikov.—1st ed.
p. cm.
Summary: Arthur and Princess Guenevere meet when they are young, and, with the help of a magical sword that appears from the middle of a lake, they fend off the advances of a band of thieves who mean to kill them.
ISBN: 978-0-525-47934-5
1. Arthurian romances—Adaptations. [1. Arthur, King—Legends. 2. Knights and knighthood—Folklore. 3. Folklore—England.] I. Oleynikov, Igor, ill. II. Title.
PZ8.1.K745Ar 2008 398.2—dc22
[E]   2007011802

Published in the United States by Dutton Children's Books, a division of Penguin Young Readers Group
345 Hudson Street, New York, New York 10014
www.penguin.com/youngreaders

Designed by Irene Vandervoort   Manufactured in China   First Edition

1 3 5 7 9 10 8 6 4 2

I N THE DAYS OF OLD, long, long ago, there were kings and knights and castles. There were princesses and dragons. There was heraldry and magic. And there was a boy named Arthur.

Arthur was the adopted son of Sir Ector and brother to Sir Kay, both brave knights, and it was with them that he went to the tournament. It was a festive place for knights to joust and boast of their bravery.

"I will one day be a knight!" said Arthur to Sir Kay.

"You, a knight?" laughed Kay. "And I suppose you are going to be king as well, hey?" He poked Arthur with his metal glove. "You're barely even a squire. You can hardly carry my shield. And you don't even know how to use it to defend yourself."

Kay snatched his shield from Arthur. "Well, Grunt, be at it. Go along and rescue a princess or something." Kay was still laughing as Arthur wandered off into the woods to be alone.

Inside the tent of King Leodegrance were a magician conjuring birds out of a hat and a minstrel playing many different instruments at once. Staring at the ground was Guenevere. She was the king's daughter—a princess! And she was completely bored. She had come along to the tournament not to watch silly performances or knights battle, but to *be* a knight in battle. Guenevere thought she was as tough and brave as any knight and sought adventure!

Guenevere had finally had enough. "I need some fresh air."

"No strolling off, m'lady," said her handmaiden Fiona.

"I promise," replied Guenevere.

But outside, she spied the woods and headed straight for them, thinking to find some adventure. She had promised not to *stroll off*, but she wasn't strolling. She was walking—very fast. And skipping.

Arthur was sitting in a tree, thinking that his brother was right. He was too small and weak to be a knight. No one would ever take him seriously. As he thought, he heard a sound. He turned and saw a girl, frolicking down the path. Now was his chance to be a true knight.

"Who goes there?" he shouted. The girl jumped, then looked up at him.

"I am Princess Guenevere. Who are you?" Arthur hopped down from his branch and bowed.

"I am Arthur…*Princess*." He laughed—she wasn't *really* a princess. "Squire to Sir Kay. I shall protect you from these woods, m'lady."

"You don't look as if you could protect a rabbit," said Guenevere with a smirk.

"Oh, yes I could," Arthur challenged.

"Not if I wanted to take it from you," Guenevere dared him.

She grabbed a rock and held two fingers above it, then tossed it at him. "There's your rabbit. Defend it!" Arthur caught the "rabbit" but dropped it as Guenevere jumped on him, sending them both tumbling to the ground. They struggled until Guenevere pulled Arthur's hair. He yelped, grabbing his head, and Guenevere triumphantly captured the "rabbit."

Arthur sat up and looked gloomily at her. "I could not best even you, a girl. I shall never be a knight."

Guenevere was pleased with her victory but didn't want to be mean. "Well, I thought you were very noble," she said.

"You did?" Arthur asked.

"Certainly. And I did pull your hair, and that's cheating, because I don't think knights really do that." Arthur was beginning to feel better.

"My friends call me Guen," said Guenevere.

They shook hands.

"Everyone calls me Arthur—except my brother. He calls me Grunt."

"Grunt?" Guen laughed. She stood up and bowed. "Pleased to meet you, Sir Grunt....That's awful!"

"Actually," said Arthur, smiling, "I don't mind it when you say it." Guen smiled, too.

But unbeknownst to Arthur and Guen, there was someone else in the woods—and he was not smiling. They could not see him; he'd made sure of that. He had been watching Arthur for some time. He stroked his long white beard and wondered why he, who could see into the future, had not foreseen this. The time was not right for them to meet. Not yet. But he remained quite still, and listened.

"Perhaps," Guen said to Arthur, "you are better at other things. I challenge you to a footrace."

Arthur smiled broadly. Here was something that he could win, for he was fleet of foot.

"I accept your…" he began.

But Guen was off like a flash through the woods. Arthur was soon close behind. Guen looked back and taunted, "You need to be faster to catch me, Sir—" *Oompf!*

Guen struck something hard and was knocked to the ground, and Arthur toppled onto her.

Arthur and Guen looked up to see the biggest, ugliest, dirtiest man they'd ever seen. "Well, well," he said in an unpleasant voice, "whot 'ave we 'ere?"

Beyond him was a whole *group* of unsavory-looking men—brigands and thieves, here to prey upon the crowds at the tournament, and Arthur and Guenevere were smack in the middle of their secret camp. There were nine of them in all, equally dirty and ugly. The big one, their leader, guffawed, "Look, men, a young lad an' lass out for a stroll." The thieves laughed. "Come to give us all your valuables then, 'ave you?"

Arthur and Guen rose shakily to their feet. Arthur stepped bravely in front of Guen to shield her. "We mean you no harm. We shall just be on our way." Guen stepped to Arthur's side. In a firm voice she said, "I am Princess Guenevere, daughter of King Leodegrance of Cameliard. I am accompanied to the tournament by great knights, and woe to you if any harm befalls us."

Arthur rolled his eyes.

"Guen," he hissed. "Stop it!"

"But I really am a princess!"

"Well…Princess…" said their leader, "we can't 'ave you spillin' our beans, so we'll 'ave to do away with you both. But first I'll be takin' those jewels." As he reached for Guen's necklace Arthur said calmly, "I think not." The bandit laughed and turned toward Arthur, who kicked him hard in the shin.

The thief hollered in pain, grabbed his leg, and toppled over. Another brigand tripped over him as he tried to grab Arthur, who ducked and crashed into a third, who fell on top of both of them. Guen grabbed a frying pan and whacked an unlucky bandit on the head. Arthur shouted, "Well done, Princess!"

"That's four down!" she declared. "What now, Sir Grunt?" The remaining thieves took up their weapons and started toward them. *"Run!"* cried Arthur.

They ran, the five angry cutthroats on their tails. Once out of sight, they hid behind a tree, and Arthur grabbed a nearby sapling and pulled with all his strength until it was bent in half. When one unwary thief, huffing and puffing, approached the tree, Arthur let go, smacking the thief and sending him flying.

"Sir Arthur, you are a fine knight indeed!" Guen said.

Arthur grinned and motioned to keep running.

The four remaining crooks chased them all the way to the lake. Arthur and Guen waded in, hoping to cross, but it was no use—they were trapped. The bandits slowly approached them with their weapons at the ready. Just as they were about to strike, the ground underfoot began to tremble…

…and in the middle of the lake a fountain sprang up.

They all stood transfixed as up from the center of the fountain stretched a lady's arm, holding a great sword, gleaming in silver and gold. The sword flew through the air right into Arthur's hand; then the mysterious arm and fountain sank back into the water and vanished.

As if the sword was made just for Arthur, he somehow knew exactly what to do. He faced the gang of now frightened cutthroats. One of them charged him. Arthur swung his magic sword with both hands and sliced the other's sword neatly in half. The thug stared at it wide-eyed for a moment, then ran off screaming like a little girl.

Another let loose an arrow, straight for Arthur's head. Arthur swung around with his sword, and the arrow bounced harmlessly off it. The thieves were scared stiff. With a wink to Guen, Arthur said, "And now, Princess, your loyal knight shall finish them." He howled and ran at them. They dropped their weapons and ran off, except for one who fainted dead away.

Arthur and Guenevere laughed and cheered. Guen took the sword from Arthur. "Kneel, Arthur." He knelt on one knee. She stood straight and tall before him. "You have acted with bravery and nobility," she said formally. "You have defended me, and do me honor. By my birthright as Princess, Heir to the King of Cameliard, with this magical sword I hereby dub thee knight." She lifted the heavy sword and touched him once on each shoulder. "Arise, Sir Arthur! . . . of Grunt!"

Arthur took the sword and held it high in triumph.

And then...Guenevere kissed him! Arthur was so stunned that he let go of his sword, and as he did, it leaped out of his hands and soared off into the sky, higher and higher until, finally, it was gone.

Sir Arthur of Grunt and Princess Guenevere knew that the time had come for them to go their separate ways.

"Thank you for making me a knight," said Arthur. "I'm sure we'll see each other again someday."

"Yes," she agreed. "You'll appear one day at the castle door and ask for my hand."

"Me, marry a princess?" said Arthur.

"You're right," she said, smiling. "I'll be a queen by then."

"Well then, I shall need to be a king. King Arthur and Queen Guenevere." They laughed.

"I shall never forget this day," said Arthur, "or you."

"Nor shall I forget you," said Guen.

"Ah, but forget you shall!" said a voice from nowhere.

Suddenly, standing there, they saw a man with a long white beard, dressed in long, flowing robes.

"I am the Wizard Merlin, guardian of the future. I am also your guardian, Arthur. I watch over you because you have a great destiny to fulfill. As do you, Princess Guenevere."

"So you did all of this, then?" said Arthur.

"Indeed not. I gave you no help, for you needed none."

"What about the magic sword?" asked Guen.

"That was not I, but the Lady of the Lake, a powerful magical being who rules the waters. Pay heed. Your destinies are intertwined. You must meet—at the proper time—and so cannot be allowed to remember this day. I shall cast a spell that will make you forget."

"I'll never forget!" shouted Arthur.

"Nor I!" added Guenevere.

"No, not entirely, 'tis true," offered Merlin calmly. "You will not forget much of what you found here today—your confidence, your bravery, your cleverness. But all else—the sword, the battles, each other, even me—you will know only in your dreams. So go, be off. Your families await you."

Guen and Arthur shared a final hug and promised they would not forget, but as they walked in opposite directions, Merlin cast his spell, and forget they did.

Back at the tournament, Arthur, somehow, felt grand. His brother said, "Where had you gotten off to, Grunt?"

"Just a walk in the woods," said Arthur. "And that's *Sir* Arthur *of* Grunt to you!"

"Sir Grunt, is it?" He threw his shield at Arthur, who caught it smartly, twirled it around, and held it firm in defense position. Before Sir Kay could speak, a group of shady characters passing by saw Arthur and, for some reason, bowed nervously. "Good day, sir" and "Pardon us, sir," they said, and then scampered quickly away.

Arthur was confused, but said to Kay, "Even they know a *sir* when they see one!"

"You know, Sir Grunt," said Sir Kay, "there may be hope for you yet."